KAWAII FA

Thank you for choosing The Colorist's Corner.

If you found this coloring book enjoyable, please leave us a review.

COLOR TEST PAGE

Color Test Page

Thank You!

Thank you for choosing the Colorist's Corner.

We truly hope you have an enjoyable experience.

Please consider leaving us a review.

Happy Coloring!

Made in the USA
Monee, IL
04 November 2024